HOOK

A FRACTURED FAIRY TALE

By

J.E. Taylor

J.E. TAYLOR
SUPERNATURAL SUSPENSE
& DARK FANTASY AUTHOR

Pirate. Villain. Gentleman?

The first time I set eyes on the scruffy rogue Elijah Hook, I wasn't sure what kind of man he truly was. But when he fought to set me free from the gilded cage the lost boys kept me in, I knew he was worthy of my attention.

When those boys found out I was smitten with the good captain, they spread the most heinous of lies. Stories so offending that the people of San Juan went on the hunt for him, intending to take him straight to the gallows.

Now, I have a choice—save Captain Hook and live at the mercy of the lost boys in Neverland for the rest of my days, or watch them kill my true love.

HOOK Chapter 1

I'VE BEEN IN CAPTIVITY for decades. Tormented and used by a bunch of entitled brats who never want to grow up. They abuse my magical abilities to keep themselves young, and to defy gravity and fly every chance they get. In my natural form in this realm, I'm slight in size, maybe four inches tall at best, and I can fit into a gentleman's hand. However, the children who hold me, and my magic, hostage are *not* gentlemen by any means.

It's a heavy burden on my magic. One that nearly drains me. It's a wonder I have survived this long, but if they keep at it, I won't see many more sunrises.

"Lilly, make me fly," Peter insists as he stands outside the cage holding me hostage. His blond hair stands in spikes, and his dark eyes look as crazed as ever.

I swear the magic keeping him under ten years old all these years has made him even more batshit crazy than he was before. They drove me too hard last night, and I just have nothing more in my magical reserves.

"I can't. I need rest."

He picks up the cage and shakes it, throwing me from side to side like a rag doll in a chariot. His prepubescent face scrunches in anger.

"Do you wish to kill me?" I yell as I tumble into the bars hard enough to leave a bruise.

The shaking stops, but his glare is more focused. "Maybe I'll pluck your wings," he snarls.

"Go ahead. Then my magic will surely be gone." I climb to my feet and dust myself off.

Peter is far worse than most of the others. He's their leader, and I guess he feels he has to show his dominance by beating up the poor, innocent fae locked in this golden birdcage.

It's ludicrous. But that's been my life since my sister ran off with another fae, leaving me to fend for myself. That lasted only a few weeks before Peter trapped me, and I've been at the boys' mercy ever since.

Unfortunately for me, not one of them has a merciful bone in their bodies.

He slams my cage on the table, dropping me to the floor with the force. I don't look up until his angry ranting fades, and I am now alone in the room. I sigh as the flood of relief makes my muscles weak. If I hadn't already been sitting on the ground, I would have fallen into a puddle of shaking flesh.

Peter and the lost boys used my magic to fly all over the island earlier, looking for a hidden treasure that doesn't exist. It's their game, one that takes all my concentration and drains me for at least a day. Then they wanted to go in search of a famous pirate who is said to have docked near one of the outer islands.

They will have to wait another day because I don't have it in me to keep them above sea level for the trek out to the desolate island. Even now, as they talk in the far room, their schemes of taking over the boat and sailing the seven seas pillaging and slaughtering entire islands, sickens me.

The pirate they speak of is renowned for both his generosity and his cunning. Even I have heard of Captain Hook. The mighty pirate who owns the high seas and rules them with an iron fist. Those who cross him disappear into the wind.

If that is true and Peter and his derelicts want to start a fight with such a man, who am I to stop them?

HOOK Chapter 2

SUN BLINDS ME AS I'm stirred awake by motion. I don't know whether it's dawn or dusk, and it takes me a moment to acclimate. The blinding sunset masks the scenery, but I think I know where Peter is headed, especially running at this speed. His favorite place to launch into flight from. The cliffs with a drop of close to one hundred feet right onto the deadliest crop of rocks I've ever seen. And I have seen them up close enough to know.

"You better wake up and get that magic flowing," he says and keeps on running.

This is par for the course. No gentle waking and stretching and a moment to tap into my power. No, this is a panic pulse every time, and it's no wonder I am exhausted afterwards. None of them would survive that fall, and I doubt I would either. The jagged rocks below would break my cage as surely as they would break all their bones. Although, I have dreamed about their cries of excitement turning to fear before the wet sound of flesh meets rock at terminal velocity.

I toss all those thoughts away and weave my magic to enable the boys to defy gravity. They swoop down in swan dives with Peter in the lead and my cage extended out in his hand. I would hit first if my magic ever failed, and the little shit always comes close to nailing the jagged rocks with my cage. At the very last second, though, he corrects his trajectory to skim over the water by mere inches before flowing back up out of reach of the sea predators.

I just concentrate on keeping them airborne while I hope he will not tax me. It's an empty hope because Peter always pushes me beyond my limit. The distance to where they are heading will likely deplete me of every ounce of my fae magic.

He heads straight toward the outer islands. Toward where they were told Captain Hook and his famous pirate ship are moored. I am sure Peter's pet crocodile uses this area as one of his hunting grounds. Somehow, that monster knows when Peter is on the hunt, and I won't be surprised to see his ugly, scarred back surface near the ship.

My grip on the tether hanging from the center of the canopy tightens at the thought of that ugly beast. That little piece of leather is the only thing keeping me from being squashed against the bars from the whipping wind.

The isle of caverns is farther out over the sea than zipping around Neverland looking for treasure. It takes all my concentration to keep the dozen boys airborne. We loop around it once, twice, and it isn't until the third pass that Peter sees a pirate's pennant almost hidden by one of the large rock formations in the sea surrounding the island.

Shadows on the deck give the impression of people, but as we get closer, there is only one man standing at the helm looking out over the waters with his back to us. The rest seem to be below. Their laughing banter filters out windows into the growing darkness.

"Lock everyone below," Peter says as we approach the man's blind side.

The wind blows at us, sending his voice back towards the island. If it had been a land breeze, Peter's words would have warned the pirate.

With the last of my magic, I spell the ship, locking the doors and stairwells leading to the deck, keeping those already below deck in place until Peter says so.

Our landing is a little rougher than usual, since I'm almost tapped out. Twelve feet slam to the deck, and the pirate turns our way. Even in the low light of dusk, his striking eyes capture my breath. I have no more energy, no more magic to keep the boys on the air currents, and I collapse onto the floor of my cage, but I cannot remove my gaze from the pirate. His unkept, shoulder-length hair is as dark as the night itself blows on the breeze, and his firm jaw is lined with a few days' worth of stubble, but not a full beard like I expected.

His lips turn down at the intrusion.

"Hook, I presume," Peter says and makes a hand signal to his little posse.

The boys fan out, searching for others while Peter pulls out his sword, aiming it at the captain.

The captain's gaze flicks from the sword to my cage and then comes to rest on Peter. He gives a single nod.

Peter lifts the cage. "Relieve the captain of his life."

It's the first time in all the years I've been at Peter's mercy that he has ordered me to kill. He's had me disarm his victims before, but not kill. That, he reserves for himself and his merry band or to the town officials for those that stand in his way.

It is against everything I am. Even if I had the magic to strip the captain of his life force, I wouldn't. Besides, something about the captain stirs a deep longing inside me I've never experienced before. I barely lift my head and deny his request with a slow shake.

Captain Hook's eyes narrow as he stares at the cage in Peter's hand. Then they grow decidedly dark as they slash to Peter. He draws his sword from the scabbard but holds it loosely at his side as his gaze moves to keep track of the others.

The boys gather around Peter in a protective stance. I will give them one thing. They are loyal to Peter to a fault. Schafer, his second-in-command and equal in his depravity, steps closer, his pudginess clearing space as he goes.

"All clear," he says, but Peter doesn't appear to be listening.

Peter glares at me and shakes the cage to get a reaction. I look away from the captain, and my chest feels like my heart's been ripped out and stomped on. I meet Peter's angry eyes and just stare at him, sapped of every ounce of energy, enough so I can't even lift my head.

"I suggest you let the lady go," Captain Hook says with a voice meant for the Gods. It has a musical timbre to it that makes my already helpless muscles even weaker.

My cage rattles as Peter stalks toward the captain. "What did you say?" he growls like an insolent child.

"I said let the lady go before you kill her." Captain Hook stands with his sword out, but not in a battle stance. At least not yet.

Peter rattles my cage. "Strike him down!" he commands.

I don't have enough energy to make the boy rise off the ground right now, and he expects me to kill a man? He is truly insane. I barely lift my head.

Captain Hook brings his sword up, pointing it at Peter. "I will only say this once more, and then I will run my sword through you. Let. Her. Go."

Peter is too occupied with shaking my cage to hear the threat. "If you don't do something, I will feed *you* to the crocodile," he screams at me. His rage fills the air like the stench of rotting seaweed.

The other lost boys have their swords pointing at the threat in front of them. The infamous pirate Captain Hook stands before them, not showing an ounce of fear. After all, these boys look like children, but he should be afraid, and I find myself wanting to warn him.

Unfortunately, I am so depleted of power that my body feels hollow and weak. Even so, the captain's gaze locks on mine, and his eyes radiate a fury so lethal that I swallow hard, thanking the Gods it isn't aimed at me.

Captain Hook steps forward.

The lost boys crowd around Peter with their swords pointing at the captain as well, protecting their leader.

"Useless fairy," Peter growls and tosses the cage.

It flips end over end beyond the edge of the boat they are trying to steal from the captain. My last ounce of power was used to lock the crew below deck, and the doors below rattle against their attempts to escape.

The dark water swirls with danger. When we took possession of the boat, Peter's crocodile, the biggest in the region, surfaced, looking for its next meal.

Peter usually delivers when he goes on the attack, and the crocodile is one fat mother because of Peter's brutality. But this time, it's not a bushel of pirates trying to capitalize on Neverland being thrown in as bait. This time, it's me flying through the air in a cage that will sink to the bottom, and I'm helplessly locked inside. I don't know how long it will take, but I'm facing death by drowning.

"What have you done?" Captain Hook's voice follows me as my cage splashes down sideways on the ocean's surface.

The clash of metal reaches my ears before the water does, and my last wish is for the captain to end Peter.

The force of the water pins me, so all I can do is watch as the cage drops under. The crocodile is there with his open smile. He races toward the cage, and my eyes bug out at the sight. My entire form trembles with fear as his mouth opens and teeth like daggers approach.

I'm not sure which death will be more pleasant. Drowning or being shish-kebabbed by those teeth. I just want it to be quick.

But that doesn't seem to be in the cards either.

The metal of the cage sticks in the crocodile's teeth. He whips his head back and forth, trying to either crush or dislodge the cage. It's only a matter of time before the metal gives under the pressure. It's already creaking. Either that, or the water rushing in and out of my ears is messing with my hearing.

A splash nearby snaps the crocodile's head in that direction.

My lungs strain for me to take a breath, and I almost give in, but then the vision of the captain swimming toward me and leaving a trail of blood behind him makes me hold on. I don't know why. His blood will surely bring other predators, ones that are bigger and badder than the old crocodile trying to kill me.

Captain Hook's gaze finds mine, and he swims harder, reaching us as the crocodile swings around to face him. He grabs the cage and flips himself on top of the beast. He then grips the gator's lower jaw, prying it open as he leverages the cage to pull its top jaw up.

He yells in the water at the strain. Bubbles blow out of his mouth, and then, suddenly, the cage springs loose, peeling a crocodile tooth out that lands next to me.

The captain's yell becomes higher pitched, one of pain versus exertion. He slams the cage against the crocodile's head, stunning both the beast and me with the motion. He launches toward shore, using the cage to claw through the water. I grab a bar and hold on, gasping for air anytime I surface.

We reach an outcrop of rock, and he climbs up, setting the cage beside him. The water behind us still has a trail of red, and I'm sure the crocodile will leap up and end us at any second. I think Captain Hook is thinking the same thing because he rips off his belt, affixes it to just above his bleeding wrist, and yanks it tight. Then he hops onto his feet and grabs the cage, jumping from rock to rock until he reaches the shore.

My heart drops at what I can see of his injury. If he doesn't get medical attention quick, he's likely to bleed out. Where his sword hand used to be is just a bloody stump. He lost his hand to the crocodile.

Captain Hook doesn't stop running at the shoreline or the edge of the jungle. He jogs until he stumbles into a small clearing and collapses onto his back with my cage centered on his chest. He holds his injured arm over his eyes as he breathes heavily below me.

If the lost boys pursue him, I don't think he has the strength to outrun them. I glance back toward shore. There are enough men aboard the captain's ship to keep their sadistic tendencies company for quite some time.

I cough water out of my lungs as I assess my own damages. Beyond a few hefty bruises from hitting the sides of the cage, I am not that bad off.

"Thank you," I whisper through my wheezing.

He just nods, but doesn't speak.

I get into a kneeling position and place my hands on the bottom of the cage. It's the closest connection to this rogue savior that I have. I close my eyes and concentrate, pulling out the last drips of magic in my reservoir. I push it out, commanding it to heal the captain.

He hisses through his teeth and uncovers his eyes to look at me. "I'll be fine. Conserve your energy," he whispers.

I've never had someone refuse my healing magic before. I pull my hands away, doing as he asks. His blue-eyed stare compels me in a way I can't explain. It heats me and energizes me. Water drips from his dark hair, and grains of sand slide off the ends back to the ground. He reaches up and pulls on the lock holding the door closed as if his hand can just crush it and free me.

But this metal is forged with dark magic. It cannot be so easily broken.

His head drops back down, and a heavy sigh leaves his body before he moves the cage to the ground beside him. Then the man reaches across his body into his far pants pocket. His face pinches in concentration. Then he frees a folded knife out from the depths of his pants. That little sticker isn't enough to fight off anything, but still, he slips it between his teeth and pulls the blade open.

With a determined set of his jaw, he slowly sits up. His face pales as he lowers his injured arm, and he closes his eyes, breathing long and slow, fighting whatever demons grip him. Color soon returns to his cheeks, but it's blotchy enough for my worry to flare.

When he puts his injured arm on the cage to steady it, I ask, "What are you doing?"

"Trying to get you out of this damn cage," he says through clenched teeth.

He jams the blade of the knife between the lock and the door. The flat blade slides in with a little effort, and then he turns it so the business end of the blade faces outward, putting pressure on the lock. The snap of metal fills the space.

My heart soars for a moment and then falls just as hard to the floor of the cage. The hilt of his knife still in his grip has a jagged and broken edge. He stares at it in disbelief.

"Damn it," he mutters, and then jams the broken blade into the same space where the rest of the knife is still stuck.

The short stub seems more resilient. His muscles flex, nearly ripping his wet shirt.

Another snap echoes, and I expect to see the hilt of his knife in pieces. Instead, Captain Hook flicks open the door and offers me his hand to climb onto.

"You are free to go." His voice sounds as drained as he looks.

His palm is warm as he moves me out from within the cage, but it has been too long since I truly took flight that my wings can't even hold my weight right now. They flutter behind me, useless.

I drop to my knee in his palm and lower my head in respect.

"I'm not a god to be revered, fae." His voice rings out over the clearing, and his eyes narrow in admonishment. "I'm just a man and certainly not one to be honored in such a way." He glances at his handless arm and lifts it for me to see. "A one-handed man at that."

"You have earned my loyalty by saving my life, Captain."

He scoffs and attempts to stand. He gets one knee under him and teeters, losing his balance. Instead of catching himself with his only hand which I occupy, he falls over on his shoulder with a wince of pain.

His cheeks redden as his gaze slices to mine. "Maybe a little healing might not be a bad idea."

"You think?" I ask with my brows raised.

I offer a smile and place my hands on his palm, concentrating. Not only has his hand been decapitated, but his thigh has a nasty slice, probably made by one of the lost boys as he jumped ship. Both wounds need addressing, so the man doesn't bleed out on me. With everything I have left, I push out my healing power, dividing it between the two injuries.

He winces, but remains still.

When the last stitch of magic inside me flows from me to him, I collapse in his palm, breathing as heavily as he is. I can't even lift my head.

"Sweet fae, did you not save anything for yourself?" he whispers as he climbs to his feet, successfully this time.

I just smile up at him. "You deserve it."

His laugh rings out like a musical symphony. "Oh, my sweet, sweet pixie. I most certainly do not deserve to be saved."

That laugh. I could ride on it forever. It's the sweetest melody I have ever heard. My smile remains on my lips, and I close my eyes.

His sigh brushes over me. After a moment, he slips me into his shirt pocket as gently as a mother tending to her child. I snuggle into the wet fabric warmed by his body heat. Leaning into him, I can hear his strong heartbeat. It soothes me, allowing my magic to regenerate. The lull of his steps, along with the steady beat of his heart, lures me into a deep slumber. One that is blissfully absent of the nightmares that usually haunt my sleep.

HOOK Chapter 3

I WAKE WITH A start in a hot, cramped space and the illusion of moving. I take a minute to get my senses in order, and to figure out just where the hell I am.

Oh yeah. Hook's pocket. I lean my ear to the inner wall of fabric encasing me, and there it is. His strong heartbeat, but I also hear his labored breathing.

Did you know it is not easy climbing fabric?

Even if I stand, I still can't reach the top to pull myself up to see over the edge of his pocket. And Captain Hook is most definitely moving. I push my back to his chest and use my legs to climb up like one would do if they were climbing up in a tight crevice. However, while my legs move up, my back doesn't, and I'm soon folded like a pretzel. I walk my feet back down to the bottom of the pocket and resign myself to being captive.

His stride slows, and the top of the pocket pulls out. "Ah, you're awake," Captain Hook says with a sexy tilt of his lips.

I should not be noticing things like that. I'm ancient compared to him. Even so, I guess being in the presence of boys has left my mind in the gutter when I am introduced to a man like Captain Hook.

"Yes. And if you please, I'd like to get out of your pocket now."

He stretches his finger into the pocket, and I grab on. With slow movements, he pulls me out and then props me on his shoulder.

"Hang on, little lady," he says and then jogs.

"My name is Lilly," I say as I grip his shirt in my fists.

After a few jarring bounces, I sync to his rhythm. His hair occasionally tickles me, but now that I'm not bucking around like some novice rider, I can study his profile a little closer. His cheeks hold the scruff of a few days without shaving; it's not a full beard like the rumors of him announce. The only thing they got right was his raven-colored hair. Oh, and his piercing blue eyes that can either freeze you in your spot or make your knees knock. What those rumors don't explain is that Captain Elijah Hook is so very swoon worthy.

I look forward quickly because just staring at his profile is making my body pliant enough to fall off his shoulder if I'm not careful.

I blink at the break in the trees and the shore beyond. "Where are you going?"

"I need to find that damn crocodile."

"But what if the boys are out there?" Fear coats my voice. I do not want to be caged again.

The captain slows his gait and glances at me. "No harm will come to you, Lilly."

I let out a high-pitched laugh. "You do not know Peter Pan. He will pluck my wings out of spite."

"My boat is no longer anchored on this side of the island." He points to the rocky outcrops and beyond at the sea.

No boats are visible, but that doesn't mean Peter can't be hiding.

"We didn't see your pirate's mast until we were almost upon you. They could easily hide behind those outcrops." I point at the rock towers shooting from the ocean like God's pillars.

"I still need to find that croc."

"Why risk your life?"

"Because that watch it stole is special, and I need it back." He presses his lips together as he studies the horizon. "Besides, I also need to find my damn sword, which is at the bottom of the ocean." He waves his good hand at the water. "I'm useless to you without it."

I close my eyes and let my magic flow through me. When I open my eyes, a watch materializes on his wrist, and an ornate sword similar to the one he had appears in his hand.

He raises an eyebrow. "The watch is...very nice." He lowers his weapon and takes a moment to study his new watch. "Extremely nice," he says with a voice that carries admiration. "And the sword is almost an exact replica, which saves me from having to search the ocean floor." He glances at me and sighs. "I do not mean to seem ungrateful, because I am so very grateful that you would waste your magic on me, but I still need to find that beast and get the watch it swallowed when it bit off my hand."

I roll my eyes at him. "A gift from a lost love?" It's the only thing I can think of to treasure.

His light laugh strikes a chord in me. I could listen to that for eternity.

"No. There is no lost love. No fair maiden waiting for me to come save her." He glances at me with humor crinkling his eyes. "It's just something I need." He doesn't explain further and keeps walking toward the waterline.

As he approaches the ocean lapping the shore, he scans the water, looking for signs of crocodiles, but there's nothing but a smooth surface, as if the mighty ocean is a calm lake.

He sighs. "Any chance you can wish that thing here so I can kill and gut it?"

I balk at him. "I'm not bringing that monster here, so it can do more harm."

Captain Hook twirls the sword around in his hand. "I am just as good with my left hand as I was with my right."

"No." I cannot let that beast near us. The captain doesn't know the thing is infused with magic, so it will attack anyone who has ill intent towards Peter. And I will say that Captain Hook has a potent reason to have ill intent towards that hellish child.

"Okay. Then I guess I'm swimming." He takes me off his shoulder and puts me on the rock before kicking off his boots. Then he unbuttons his shirt with one hand while I gawk at him.

I cannot believe he is going to go looking for trouble.

Then his pants drop.

And I'm the one suddenly in trouble. I am helpless to avoid looking at the hard lines of his muscles. He is exquisitely cut. A life as a sailor requires hearty souls, and he certainly qualifies with his hard abs, wide shoulders, and tapered waist. As he walks to the water, the muscles in his fine ass mock me with their perfection.

He glances over his shoulder as if he can feel my eyes scanning his heavenly form. The smile he flashes nearly has me swooning. But then he dives under the water, disappearing from view. My heart falls at my feet, and it's replaced by the heat of sheer panic.

I flutter my wings, muttering under my breath at the lack of strength in them. They don't even lift me up a fraction of an inch. Flying to where bubbles are surfacing will not work. I glance around me. I'm just as exposed here to predators as he is out in the ocean.

Captain Hook's head pops up out of the water before he stands. His hair drips as he surveys the area, and then he turns and trudges back to shore with a look of utter disgust on his face. He throws the sword on the ground and then pulls on his pants, muttering about not being able to swim and hold the sword at the same time.

He takes a seat next to me and pulls his boots on, but he doesn't put his shirt on, and I can't say I'm disappointed. His defeat stains the air, and he leans his arms on his knees and drops his head into the crook of his elbow.

"Captain?"

He turns his head toward me. "Please call me Elijah."

I lick my lips and try out his name. "Elijah." It feels like silk across my tongue, and a foreign heat grips me. It's as if the captain's warded with some sort of fae elixir.

A smile temporarily replaces his frustration. "I wish you were human-sized and not so tiny. Then I wouldn't be so concerned about leaving you on the beach alone."

Something shuffles behind us. Elijah grabs me and his shirt in one swipe of his hand and launches towards the tree line. He slides behind a bush and tries not to make another sound. He puts me on a branch in front of him and slips on his shirt before collecting me in his hand again.

We peek between the branches as the noise becomes loud enough to warrant the six figures that break out of the jungle on the far side of the beach.

Peter and a couple of the boys step out onto the shore on the other side, along with a half dozen authorities from the mainland. He points out toward the water and then back near where we are hiding.

My gaze falls to the sand and the captain's sword sitting there along with the boot prints leading right to where we are. That's not good. At least they are far enough away to not be able to make them out yet. I need to make both the sword and his footprints disappear.

Closing my eyes, I conjure up a gale-force wind to whip sand from our side of the beach towards the group trudging towards the water. It's strong enough to wipe away the captain's footprints, and with a little extra push, I make the sword disappear and reappear nested into the scabbard on his waist.

Captain Hook glances down at the sudden weight on his hip. His eyebrows rise, and then he glances at me with a nod of thanks. He retrieves me from the branch and slides me into his shirt pocket. Then he is moving once again, but even to my fae ears, it's as silent as a human can possibly be, almost as if he's a ghost floating over the land.

He keeps going until his feet are sloshing.

"Hold your breath, Lilly," he says in a whisper.

And then a moment later, we submerge. I'm plastered to the bottom of his shirt pocket as he moves through the water. Just when I think I can't hold my breath any longer, he takes a great inhalation of air and pulls himself out of the water.

I sputter into the wet fabric as I try to sit up. His hand reaches into the pocket and scoops me out into the damp air. Darkness surrounds us.

"Where are we?"

"In a cave I found when the tide was out. It's not accessible when it's high tide like right now." He shifted on the rock. "I also don't know if there are predators in here."

I wave my hand in an arc, sending fairy lights across the expanse. The cave lights up, and on the far side from where the captain is perched is a dry patch of beach that seems big enough for the captain to stretch out.

"You seem to have recovered your magic." He places me on his shoulder and slides into the water, and then he cuts through the water slowly, almost leisurely.

"It's easy when I'm not using it to keep a group of old men looking as if they are children and making them fly on a daily basis." I give him a push toward shore in the form of a wave just to show him what I am capable of.

When he climbs ashore, he takes his boots off and dumps out the water, and then he sets them aside to dry. He puts me on the sand, takes his shirt off, and hangs it on a nearby rock. He glances around at the shore, studying the sand.

"What are you doing?"

He smiles. "Making sure there are no crocodile markings."

I look around as the heat of fear wraps around me.

"It's clear. This cave doesn't allow for sunbathing, so we have that going for us." He takes a seat on the cool sand next to me. "Thank you for the lights, but you may want to dim them. They might reflect on the other side of the cave."

I pull back some of the magic, lowering the light enough to still see, but not enough to create a glow through the water. "How long was I out?"

He lets out a laugh. "I've been exploring this little patch of land for two days."

I stare at him, my eyes widening. "Two days?"

He nods. "I found a freshwater spring and some mango trees yesterday and had my fill. I checked on you from time to time, and you snore like a sailor." He grins at me. "I didn't figure on anyone coming looking for me. Certainly not that brat."

"Peter doesn't like to leave loose ends." I wrap my arms around myself and shudder, frowning at the thought.

The captain grunts and then stretches out next to me on his back. When he glances my way with those alluring blue eyes, my breath seems to suck from my lungs.

"I still wish you were human-sized like you were in the land of fae," he mutters under his breath.

I blink, and then my eyes widen at him. "You've been to the land of the fae?"

Humans are not allowed in our realm unless they've done something terrible and are brought in to stand trial, or have laid their life on the line for a fae and are being celebrated for their bravery.

Elijah Hook transported to our realm? I bet he saved someone important.

"Yes, I have been to the fae realm."

His tone catches me off guard. It screams criminal versus hero, and my jaw drops.

"I was young, poor, and incredibly foolish. I'm still trying to right those wrongs." He smiles at me and shrugs.

"You were bad?" It shouldn't surprise me the way this news does. After all, he's an infamous pirate, and the rumors of Captain Hook's escapades are spread far and wide. But after spending a small amount of time with him, I cannot see him being a criminal.

"I was naughty." The way his eyes sparkle and his lips tilt into a grin melts my insides.

I only remember a handful of humans paraded through our palace, but it was so long ago that none of them could possibly be the good captain. Besides, I would remember a man like him if he graced the halls of our palace while I was there.

"Were you ever naughty as a child?" he asks with a teasing tone, turning to prop his head on his good hand.

I sigh and meet his gaze. "I ran away from home with my sister."

If that didn't scream naughty, I don't know what would.

His smile fades. "Why did you run away?"

With his full interest focused on me, I find it hard to articulate the reasons I left a life as a princess to explore the realms.

"Because I wanted to discover the magic of the different realms, and my father said both my sister and I were too young for such foolishness." Oh, how I wish I had heeded his warnings. "Once we got to this realm, it was clear we were at a disadvantage being so small. If we had stayed in the forest where the ley lines were, I think we would have been fine, but we wanted to explore more of this beautiful landscape."

"So, you saw the world."

I nod. "I was as bored in that little location as I had been at home, and my sister had found her heart. They didn't want to seek adventure like I did." I chew my bottom lip and shrug. "I wasn't worldly enough to understand just how evil a child who never wanted to grow old could be." I glance at my fidgeting hands. "My adventure ended as abruptly as it began the day Peter trapped me in that cage." I wave at my wings. "I haven't flown in decades. These things don't work right now."

"Well, we'll have to work on that."

I chuckle. "My muscles are so atrophied, I'm not sure I'll ever fly again."

"Come on. It'll be an adventure." His laugh rings out in the cave, echoing against the walls. His voice is full of mirth as he gives me a side-eye.

His laugh is infectious, and I smile at him as my blood warms into a hot mess. I want an adventure with this man, and he wants to see me in a comparable package to his. Who am I to deny him?

I close my eyes, willing my form into human size as opposed to the miniscule fae package that I'm locked into here. Magic swirls around me as I concentrate. It's not as easy to do as I imagined. I haven't had magic in reserve for years, but the two-day rest gives me a reservoir to tap.

My bones and muscle stretch, snapping through the fabric covering me. The sand shifts next to me, almost ruining my focus. When everything settles into place, my eyes open.

The captain gawks at me, blinking like I'm not really in front of him. His gaze rakes over my entire form like a caress. His pupils dilate and his cheeks flush, and then he seems to regain his faculties. He reaches down for his shirt and offers the garment to me.

I stare at the fabric hooked on his index finger, but I ignore it the minute my gaze meets his. Heat fills me, pooling low in my belly at the raw want in his eyes. I step closer.

He makes a noise in his throat, something between a growl and a groan, and then he licks his lips. "I suggest you put on my shirt before I again do something very, very stupid." His voice is gruff, and his eyes plea with me to do as he asks before we cross a line that is forbidden.

I attempt to swing the shirt over my back, but my wings prevent me from putting the shirt on like a normal human.

His lips tilt into a devilish smile, and his eyes glint with mischievous intent as he watches me. After a couple futile attempts and his snort of a laugh, I hand him back the fabric while my body thrums with the same electricity that fills the surrounding air.

"If I didn't know better, I would think you were purposely teasing me." His gaze slowly lowers and then rises back to mine. "But I know fae have no sense of modesty."

He steps forward and holds the shirt to my chest, and the instant his knuckles scrape my skin, my body reacts in the most delicious way. I place my hand on top of his, stopping his movement. I do not want to hide my form from him. Warmth pools inside me when his gaze jumps to mine. I step closer, and his hand trembles.

"Lilly," he says in a soft warning.

I cannot help it. Something about him draws me closer. I want to taste his soft lips.

"Elijah," I answer, ignoring the warning in his voice.

His hand drops the shirt and moves to cup my cheek. "You are still innocent," he whispers, as if convincing himself more than me. But he pulls me closer, wrapping his handless arm around my back, drawing me in.

"And you *are* an adventure."

His lips twitch into a smile, and then a soft and silky laugh escapes him. "Oh, sweet pixie. I have dreamed of you all my life."

Before I can speak, his lips descend on mine. His hand threads through my short locks, holding my head in place as his tongue swipes across my lips.

His kiss weakens my knees, and I gasp at the sensations traveling through my form as his tongue tangles with mine in a sensual dance. The contours of his body mold to me as if we are meant to be.

I sigh with bliss.

Captain Hook pulls away from me as if I am fire incarnate, and he stumbles, falling on his butt on the sand. "I'm sorry," he whispers, as if he committed the worst sin in the universe. "I shouldn't have kissed you."

His words rush from his mouth as his gaze finds mine, begging for forgiveness.

I step back, struck by his panic. Blinking, I stutter, "D-did it not please you?"

He goes to wipe his face with his sand-covered hand and stops. He snaps his hand to get the grains off, and then he wipes the remaining sand off on his pants before he meets my gaze. "It's not that it didn't please me." His cheeks redden. "It pleased me to the core. But it is forbidden."

I slowly lower to my knees on the sand. He is right. Fae law prohibits humans and fairies from having relationships. It's the fastest way to be exiled from the fae realm. But I have been gone so long, it's as if I am already exiled.

I look up at Elijah and scoff at the old ways. Desire floods my mind and my judgement. With that kiss, Elijah Hook blew through a door I thought had been locked forever. Need wraps around me like a python, squeezing reason right out of my head.

"But we are not within the fae realm." I tilt my head, allowing a smile to form. "And here in the human realm, those rules don't apply," I purr, and crawl toward him.

"Lilly, you don't understand." He puts his hand out to stop me.

Suddenly, I'm unsure that he feels the same energy between us.

I pause as a horrifying thought fills me. "Do you not want me?"

The way his gaze melts moves me forward. I don't wait for him to deny what his eyes reflect and what sizzles in the air between us.

"Lilly," he groans as I crawl over his lap and wrap my legs around his waist, but he doesn't stop me when I press my lips to his, resuming the sweetness of his mouth mingling with mine.

Our tongues dance in a languid ballet. My wings flutter behind me, stretching as his kiss sends heat all the way to my toes. My toes and wings curl in response.

Elijah groans and grabs my shoulder, pushing me back. His breath heaves like mine. "Stop before I can't." His eyes flash wildly as he focuses on mine.

"What if I don't want to?" I pout.

I enjoy kissing Elijah. It brings such heat to my insides, and it feeds my powers like a dozen nights of deep sleep.

His gaze narrows. "Have you ever been with a man?"

The way he asks is layered with something dangerous, like an adventure I will never recover from. I shiver at the edge in his tone and shake my head.

He moves me closer until I can feel a hard shaft between us. I wiggle against him, and he grips my hip, stilling me.

"If you continue, I will shatter your innocence, and damn my soul forever." He removes his hand from my hip and lightly traces my lips with his fingers. "And as much as a part of me wants to do just that, it would not only shatter your innocence, but shatter your honor as well, and I cannot do that. No matter what *I* want."

His voice is husky and low, filled with a need so deep it must hurt as much as it hurts me. His finger lingers on my lips, and then he meets my gaze with the barest of smiles.

"I don't understand." I search his eyes for answers, but all I see is his desires.

"Someday you will thank me for being a gentleman." He leans forward and captures a chaste kiss before shuffling back a little.

I don't make it easy for him to disengage. Not with my pride hurting so much by his denial.

"You are more than beautiful, Lilly, and I would be a lucky man to capture your heart. But I will not ruin you, despite my desiring you in every way." He climbs to his feet and puts distance between us. "If…"

He seems unwilling to finish his sentence. He takes a running start and dives into the water, and then he surfaces in the middle of the cavern's pool. He treads water for a few minutes before he makes his way back to shore.

I snap back into my normal form and find solace under his crumpled shirt so I can hide my tears as the despair of his rejection settles in my bones.

HOOK Chapter 4

WE WAIT IN AWKWARD silence. Neither one of us is willing to breach the chasm that is wedged between us. Elijah rests with his eyes closed, but he's not sleeping and neither am I. Tension fills the cavern, and my lights blink in and out as my magical connection rises and falls with my emotions.

When the tide reaches its lowest point, Elijah puts his shirt on and offers me his hand. The silence that has befallen us is thicker than the knots in my stomach. So, his offer to take me with him is surprising.

I stare at the offered palm and then glance up at him. "Why do you want me with you?"

"I am not leaving you to be captured by that little brat again. Come on. It's time to find that crocodile." Even with the conviction in his words, his eyes still hold hesitation as if I might be poison to him. "Besides, we still have to get you flying with those wings so you can get back to that ley line and your home realm." He tilts his lips into a smile.

I ignore his attempt at levity and focus on the more pressing issue. "The crocodile is likely wherever your ship and Peter are."

"Then it's time to get my ship back and free my crew."

My stomach sinks. His crew is likely at the bottom of the ocean or in the creature's stomach. Peter never leaves his captives alive. I step into the captain's palm, and he brings me to eye height.

"What is it?" He searches my gaze.

"Peter isn't one to let those he captures live. Especially when he wants your boat."

He pales as he looks at the opening of the cave and then walks with purpose. He sets me on his shoulder next to his tight jaw, and just before I remove the fairy lights, I see a sheen in his eyes that wets his lashes. But then the lights go out, and I lose sight of his hidden sorrow.

When we step out into the fading daylight, his eyes are filled with resolve. Instead of heading toward the beach, he climbs up the hill to the highest point on the island. I remain quiet as we crest the rocky top above the tree line.

The captain scans the water in the light of the rising moon. He turns in a slow circle, surveying the island and the waters beyond. On the south side, the island of San Juan sits in the distance, and over the chain of islands flowing all the way out to where we stand, a crescent moon poises over the water.

"I need to get back to the mainland." He sighs as we study the scenery. "And I'm not sure I can swim that distance with my sword." He touches the sword I gave him at his left hip, caressing the handle as if it has become his most prized possession.

I laugh because swimming in these predator-infested waters is a lunatic thought. "The water is unsafe."

"I have to try, but I will have to leave the sword and my boots behind. They'll only weigh me down."

He's contemplating a swim in an environment where he is not the apex predator. Elijah is one man as opposed to almost a dozen boys. It should be easier, and I still have the tingle of magical reserves inside me.

"I can bring you."

He plucks me off his shoulder and brings me to eye level as he shakes his head. "I don't think so. I do not wish to tire you to the point of collapse like you were after you flew those boys to my boat."

"You won't tax me to the point of no return like they routinely did."

"Are you telling me that doing a trip like that will not tire you out?" His eyebrow cocks, and his skepticism bleeds through.

I glance at the distance, annoyed at his lack of faith in me. "It will tire me out, but not to the point of collapse. I trust you will let me rest afterwards." I cross my arms and purse my lips.

He graces me with a soft smile. "I can swim it."

He starts down the southern slope of the mountain into the trees, but they end abruptly to a sheer-faced cliff that drops off at what looks like a hundred feet or better. If it had been fully dark, Captain Hook may have stepped off the cliff before realizing the dark gap before him was a drop.

"Damn." He sighs and gives me a side-eye.

I gather fists full of his shirt and smile at him. "Step off."

"Not with you on my shoulder. You could easily get thrown off by the wind, and then we'd both fall to our deaths." He takes me from his shoulder and places me in his pocket, but he makes sure the fabric is wrapped around my front and beneath my armpits and my arms are outside of the edge. "You'll have a better grip this way."

I clamp down with my elbows, making the fit tighter. While my feet dangle, I can brace them against his chest if I need to.

Elijah tucks his shirt into his pants and glances down at me. "I'm trusting you to set me down on the ground safely."

He takes a deep breath and steps off the cliff.

Gravity nearly sucks me out of the shirt pocket, and my heart jumps into my throat. If I had been on his shoulder, I would have lost my grip and tumbled with him to the forest floor.

Elijah's hand covers me, holding me in place. After the initial shock of falling, magic swirls around us in the same panicked way it did when Peter jumped off the cliff to fly. I slow our descent and then, just as we reach the treetops, I propel us forward. Even though the captain just wanted to be lowered to the ground, I am not allowing him to swim those channels between islands.

"Lilly, what are you doing?" he asks.

His hand remains over me, making sure I can't slip out. It's gentle yet firm, and for the first time in a very long time, I feel safe.

"We are flying, Captain." I swoop us lower and over the water on the outside line of the islands.

If Peter is keeping watch, going the direct route would put us in view of his spyglass.

"I can see that, my little sprite. But I thought I told you just to bring me to the land below the cliff." His breath falls over me in a warm stream.

"You did. But I thought you might enjoy this experience."

"Ah. Another adventure of yours." This time, his voice sounds lighter, but he doesn't quite agree that he is enjoying himself.

I glance up and catch a dazzling smile as the captain looks out over the ocean as if this is the most natural thing in the world. We dip down lower, and I jerk my gaze forward, readjusting our height. I do not want to be within reach of a shark or crocodile in the dark waters below.

"If this is tiring you, I can swim," he says.

The joy he tries to hide from me is worth tiring me out. I fly us higher in the air, taking him on a merry ride of ups and downs and banks and swirls until he finally, blissfully laughs. It's a full laugh that takes years off his face, making him look familiar in a haunting way.

I refocus my concentration away from the captain and his captivating smile. If I don't, we'll end up hitting the water, and that would kill the adventure in a wet blink.

By the third island, my energy levels fall lower than I expect. It's not like the captain weighs more than a dozen boys, but perhaps it's because I used my magic to light the cave and to grow to human size for a while. I didn't take a nap after I returned to normal;

instead, I stewed on the captain's rebuff of my advance.

I can't fault him. Especially since he's trying to preserve my honor, and from my sister's experiences, I understand just how important a woman's honor is. But rejection still burns.

I force out the magic needed to make it to the mainland, and when we finally reach a remote beach as far away from Neverland as possible, I drop us down in the sand. The landing isn't smooth. The captain takes a couple of abrupt steps and somersaults, and then he jumps up on his feet as if he is trained in bobbled landings.

My body drains of energy, and I slide into his pocket, exhausted.

Captain Hook scoops me out of his pocket, and his sigh ruffles my hair. "This is why I did not want you to waste your magic on me. Those dark circles are back under your eyes, and you need rest." He glances around and then looks at me. "You rest while I try to find out information about my ship."

"It's either moored at the town dock or at Neverland." I struggle to push out the words as I lie in his palm.

"And where are we in relation to the town dock?" He raises an eyebrow at me.

I frown and look away.

"You do not need to protect me from those boys."

I roll my eyes at him. "As if you received that leg wound on your own."

He chuckles and turns a different shade of red than I've ever seen him. "Actually..." He winces. "Not my finest moment, but I was in a hurry to get to you. So, technically, it was self-inflicted, and the very reason I dropped the damned sword."

His suaveness drops a peg or two in my head, but that only endears him to me more. I smile up at him.

"If I had stayed aboard my ship, my crew would be alive, and Peter and his band of terrorists would be fish bait. But I would have lost you."

The melancholy in his voice squeezes my heart, but he underestimates the lost boys. I cannot let him walk into a bloodbath without warning him of their prowess.

"They are vicious things and talented with swords. I think you are not seeing them for what they are. Men trapped in boys' bodies with decades of fighting experience."

He gives me a knowing smile. "I've bested twenty very skilled men who set out to kill me." He nods to his right arm. "And all I received was a minor scratch on my shoulder. I am very adept at sword fighting, my dear. With or without my right hand." He wiggles the fingers of the hand holding me.

"But you cannot defend from both sides anymore."

He lifts his arm, staring at the space where his hand once was. "Well, then, I shall weaponize this arm to even out the odds." He gives me a cheeky grin. "Now, if you would be so kind as to point me in the right direction, I can settle you into my pocket so you can get some rest."

I don't want to direct him, but I have no choice. I point to our right and allow him to get me settled in his pocket before he sets out on his way to get his ship back.

The lull of his steps pulls me into an exhausted stupor, but I'm wired enough not to fall into the black of sleep. I'm somewhere in between when a clamor of many people talking brings me around.

The scent of spirits and drunkenness filters through the captain's pocket, and his motion ceases. A chair scrapes against wood, and then his weight shifts.

"What can I get you?" a harsh voice snaps from the space in front of us.

"Information." The captain's voice has an edge to it I haven't heard before. It carries enough danger to make me quiver.

"Information costs."

The captain moves his arm, and a moment later, something jingles onto the counter.

Did he just bargain the watch I gave him for information?

"That should be more than enough."

The rattle of metal being picked up follows. "Hmm. What is it you want to know?"

"I'm looking for my ship. The *Joli Rouge*."

"And who might you be?" the voice asked, seemingly closer than before.

"The captain of said ship." There is a smile in the captain's voice, but it still has that edge that hints if this person isn't careful, the captain will end up cutting him.

"Why aren't ya' on it, then?"

A thump on the counter makes me jump.

"I had a bit of an accident with a crocodile when I went for a swim, and I seemed to have lost sight of the boat."

A whistle follows, but no words come. Instead, a plunk of weighted glass on wood rings out. "It's on the house, Captain." Glass slides across the bar. "And I believe I heard a new ship was moored in town."

His voice carries a smile, but he doesn't tell the captain anything we don't already know.

"Thank you," Elijah says and then takes a swig of the offered spirits.

He drains the glass in one long pull. Then he slams the glass down on the bar and wipes his mouth with his shirt sleeve, still staring at the bartender. I have enough of a view to see the captain's face go slack.

"You son of a…"

That's all he gets out before his eyes roll back in his head and he collapses forward onto the bar, pinning me in place against his chest.

I use the last of my magic to push him to his side and give me some breathing room. Otherwise, his weight will crush me.

Someone lifts the captain's body and moves him to a room where no noise from the bar penetrates.

"You'll bring me a pretty penny, Captain." The bartender snickers, and chains rattle. Before the door closes, he tells someone to go get the authorities, and then all sound subsides.

My magic is tapped out. I need at least a day's rest to rejuvenate, and I curse my need to show off for Elijah. If I just let him swim, I wouldn't be this useless waif hidden in his pocket.

An hour later, the creak of a door filters around me, and the noise from the bar follows.

"You've done well."

I freeze at that voice and shake against the captain's unconscious form. Peter has found me, and I am helpless against his wrath.

HOOK Chapter 5

A SMALL HAND SLIDES into the pocket and encloses around me. The burn of the iron ring makes me gasp, and then I am free from the pocket and staring into the angry eyes of the leader of the lost boys: Peter Pan.

Two burly men stand behind Peter wearing officer uniforms. Peter has a dagger pressed to the captain's chest, and he gives me such a dark look that my mouth dries in fear.

"You don't have to speak. I'm sure it's been an awful experience being the captain's captive," Peter says to me.

His eyes are full of malice, and the warning is clear. If I deny what he says, whether or not the authorities are here, he will kill the captain.

I nod helplessly as the stench of my burning flesh surrounds me. The little shit wore that ring with the purpose of hurting me.

Peter steps away from Elijah, pocketing the knife before turning to the authorities. "Take him away."

The men each take one of the captain's arms and lift his unconscious form from the chair. His legs have mean-looking shackles that rattle as they drag him away.

The door closes, and now it's just Peter and me.

"Please don't hurt him," I beg.

His eyes narrow. "It's not up to me. He'll be tried for his crimes."

"He has done nothing!" But as soon as the words fall from my lips, I know it doesn't matter. Peter has spun his lies once again.

"Oh, is that so?" He stares me down. "According to some very reliable sources, the captain abused a lot of boys in the most heinous of ways and then stole their fae to keep as his own captive. He's killed, maimed, murdered, all in the name of piracy." Peter grins. "Your good captain should be sentenced before the sun sets."

My chest squeezes hard enough for me to choke. He must see my pain because he laughs.

"Please, I'll do anything if you set him free." My desperation bleeds through with every word.

His laugh fades, and he stares at me, rubbing his jaw as my words sink in. "Anything?"

I nod. I know what they do with criminals in this land. They hang until they are no longer alive or are flayed to death at a post for the entire community to watch. Peter has sent too many people to their deaths with his lies, and he glories in the brutality of the punishments. I swear, if he had a choice, he would be the one swinging the whip. I don't want to see Elijah killed for saving me.

Peter reaches into a bag on the floor by the door and pulls out another cage. This one is smaller and has chains hanging from the top and on the floor. "Promise me you will always serve the lost boys." He caresses my wings in a way that makes my stomach roll.

"Only if you promise to set Elijah free."

His eyebrow rises, and he seems to consider my request. Just when I think he is going to ignore my plea, he nods.

"He will be set free if you agree to my terms."

I slowly nod.

He clucks his tongue. "Say the words."

"As long as you set Elijah free, I will serve the lost boys until the day the Gods come and take me away," I say, binding myself to this sniveling man-child.

He sets the cage on the table and dumps me next to it. "Enter, and put the chains on."

I balk at him even though I know damn well I have no choice. My reserves are tapped, and with his damn iron ring, he's stunned my magic enough so I cannot reach it to save myself from this savage.

"Then I guess it's death for the good captain." He crosses his arms.

I growl and march into the cage, and then I clasp my feet first and a single arm. "There. Are you satisfied?" I snap.

He reaches in and clasps my other wrist before he closes the door on me with a smile. "Fully."

"Now follow through on your promise."

"Just as soon as I have you tucked away in Neverland. It would be quicker if you made me fly."

My eyes water. "I don't have enough magic right now." My chin trembles as tears tumble down my cheeks in hot paths, dripping onto the cage's floor where they sizzle. I gasp at the iron coin on the floor. "And you have iron in here. You know iron saps my magic."

He grins evilly. "So, we are walking." He strolls out of the door and out a back hallway into the morning light.

If I had caught some sleep, I may have been able to make him fly part of the way, but now it will take hours while the captain's fate is left to chance.

THE SUN IS LOW on the horizon as Peter waltzes into the Neverland manor. My heart runs on overdrive as my muscles cramp from being in this position. At least I can fan my wings, working on strengthening those muscles.

His crew lounges in the great room, but the minute he crosses toward the kitchen, they are up and following with interest. They don't look like prepubescent brats any longer. Now they look more like they are hitting puberty. Schafer looks as if he may have the beginnings of fine hairs growing on his upper lip. Bo seems to have shot up almost as tall as Peter, and his dark complexion is now riddled with pimples. Quinn looks uncomfortable in his too-small clothing. The others behind them look like they suffer from the same type of peculiarities.

When Peter places me on the kitchen table, I get a good look at him, bathed in sunlight. He's transitioned to a young teenager as well. His eyes darken as they take me in.

Before anyone can speak, he holds up his hand. Quiet reigns over the room.

He points at me. "You need to reverse whatever this is." He waves at himself.

I bite my lip and stare at him before I open and close my mouth. My magic has not regenerated yet.

"I need a night of rest before I have the magic to do that." I stare him down. "But you need to follow through on your end of the bargain."

I raise an eyebrow. I'm not using any magic for him and these brats until Elijah is free.

"What bargain?" Schafer demands.

Peter spins around to face them, turning his back on me. "We need to head to town to ensure they set the captain free."

"What?" Bo and Quinn say at the same time.

The shock on their faces makes me shift my weight, especially when Peter raises his hand, demanding their attention.

"I promised Lilly," he says. "And in return, she bound herself to me until her last breath."

His smugness rubs me wrong, as do the grins that form on the boys' faces as they look at Peter and then turn their leers on me.

"Let's go set the good captain free," Peter says and heads toward the door.

The clan parts, letting him lead, and then falls into place behind Peter.

I stare after them as uneasiness layers over me. Alone, I question my judgement and wonder if I've just made another colossal mistake.

DARKNESS SWALLOWS ME AS I wait for the boys to return. The chains keep me from resting, and no matter how hard I try to break free, all it does is chafe my wrists and ankles. The longer they are gone, the more my chest feels like it's being squeezed in a vise.

The door opens, and lanterns lead the way through to the kitchen where I wait. The boys head into the great room and throw themselves onto the couches, laughing at their prowess. But they aren't talking loud enough for me to pick up their conversation.

Peter crosses to the kitchen. "The captain is free."

He brings me to the window and points to a shadow crossing the harbor, heading to the open waters of the Caribbean. It's too dark to see the mast and Elijah's colors, but the size of the boat seems right.

I sag with relief and give Peter a nod.

His wicked gaze turns to me. "Now reverse our age back to what it was a few days ago."

I huff at his demand. "I need rest."

"We gave you some time to rest." His eyes narrow. "Are you going back on your bargain?"

"No, Peter. I need sleep, and I can't very well sleep chained like this." I rattle the binds holding me in place. "Unchain me so I can lie down."

He lets out a harsh laugh. "Not while he's still within reach." He nods toward the window as he brings me back to the table. "You better figure out a way to gather enough power to reverse this, or you'll be in that room with us tomorrow evening and every evening until you turn the clock back." He points to the great room as a knock on the door sounds. "Power up while we let off some of these crazy teenage hormones."

He sets me back down, but before he closes the kitchen door, I glimpse a couple of prostitutes entering the great room. The boys snicker at them before Peter sends me a knowing smile. He shuts the door, but the carnal noises that filter through are enough to leave me dreading the morning.

HOOK Chapter 6

PETER YANKS THE CAGE forward, jerking me as he walks. "Rise and shine, fae!"

The cuffs binding me tugs on my wrists and ankles, bringing me to a painful waking state. I'm surprised I finally fell asleep in this position, but apparently, I did. Even with the blanket covering the cage, the sunshine seeps through as he walks, swinging me by his side. The damned iron coin is still glued to the bottom of the cage, sapping my strength.

My brain isn't all that fast this morning as everything that happened yesterday seeps slowly back. I agreed to Peter's terms, and he made good on his promise, binding me to him until my very last breath. A part of me withers and dies at the thought that Elijah set sail without me. But his freedom is worth every ounce of pain I shall endure for the rest of my life serving Peter.

The blanket keeping me blind rips away, and my heart drops at the sight of the executioner standing on a platform with his mighty blade. The rest of the platform is empty, save for the square stump bloodied by prior beheadings.

A crowd gathers around us as Peter takes the spot right in front of the stump.

My stomach cramps. The platform will not be empty for long. Peter holds my cage up so I have a clear view, which weakens my knees.

He's never brought me to a public execution. He has always left me to see the damage from a distance, afraid that I might intervene and ruin his fun. The way the boys gush over the gruesomeness of it always makes me physically ill.

Today is different. Peter has me here for a reason. Dread creeps in like a wet fog, and I quake under the weight of it. My mind is not allowing the truth to sink in. But it's shoved right at me the moment the doors to the right of the platform open.

Everything inside of me grows cold. Elijah Hook is paraded out onto the stage half naked, with his arms bound behind him in such a way to hold them in place even without his hand. His lip bleeds, and the bruises on his face and torso look fresh enough for me to understand exactly what happened when the boys came to town last night.

Peter brings my cage up, even with his face. "Like my work?" He smiles. "We were given some time with your friend last night."

I cannot take my eyes away from Elijah. I cannot breathe. But I say, "You lied."

The kicker is I should have known better.

"Maybe now you will understand the price for crossing me."

I turn to him and narrow my eyes. Anger blooms in my chest, spiraling through me like a tornado, wiping out an entire village. Tricking the fae comes at a hefty price, and iron or not, he will soon know the depths of my wrath.

"Besides, technically, he will be free. Just not the type of free you were expecting."

Hatred flares, mixing with the already dangerous fury building in my slight form. I let it grow unchecked.

The guards force Elijah to his knees and push his head down on the stump.

A small man who reminds me of an underhanded tax man with a top hat steps out from behind the guards and lifts a scroll. "For your crimes against the children of Neverland." He waves toward the lost boys and then reads from the scroll again. "And for those crimes committed on the high seas, Captain Elijah Hook, we sentence you to death by beheading."

"What crimes?" a gruff voice shouts from the back, and Elijah searches the crowd for the source.

"Heinous crimes," the little balding man says with a frown, but he doesn't expand on them. He looks at Peter as if looking for confirmation, though.

Elijah's gaze finds me in front of the crowd and locks on mine. His lips press into a thin line as he glares at Peter and then returns his gaze to me. His anger is replaced with a sadness so deep it fuels my rage. Iron or no iron, my magic will not be contained by this imp reveling in the captain's pain.

The executioner steps up to the stump and raises the blade. It glimmers in the sunlight. I close my eyes and wish to be human size again. The binds holding my wrists and ankles tear like they are made of paper, and my body snaps into adult size in a blink, annihilating the cage with a bang that diverts everyone's attention to me.

The whistle of the blade cutting the air stops.

Hushed whispers follow. I stand naked in the town square with my wings fluttering with the wrath I can hardly contain. Magic blasts outward, claiming all that I have given to these terrorists over the years.

The blade lingering over the captain's throat evaporates like it's made of smoke, and so do the binds holding Elijah in place.

"Elijah Hook has done no harm to these villains!" I wave towards Peter and the rest of the lost boys gathered behind him. "They have terrorized for decades and shifted the blame to others. They have caged me, demanding that I keep them young. Well, that ends today. I will not be a victim of their cruelty any longer, and I will not allow Captain Hook to be murdered for their sins."

I spin on Peter and point my finger at him, feeling vindicated as my magic flows back into my form, filling me with even more power. The bastard and his friends age from young teenagers to old men in a manner of seconds.

"Peter Pan is the one whose head should be on that chopping block. Not Elijah Hook. Peter has been the one who has stolen from all of you." My voice echoes over the silent crowd. "He is the trickster who has terrorized Neverland for as long as you can remember."

My wings spread, and the crowd moves back.

Peter growls at me, but I am no longer afraid. Not with decades of power funneling back to its source. It's almost too much magic, but I breathe it in as if it is my life's blood.

Peter steps closer and brings his right fist back, and then he launches it towards my face. Before I can bring my arm up to deflect his punch, a hand darts into my view, stopping Peter's fist from connecting. I look to my side and see Elijah with Peter's fist in his, his face contorted with a deadly fury. He shoves with all his strength.

Peter stumbles backwards and trips over his own aged feet. He lands with an exhale of air and swivels his glare back on us.

"You will not lay a finger on her. You understand?" The growl in Elijah's voice echoes over the crowd as the lost boys surround us.

"She stole my youth!" Peter points at me, and then his eyes widen. He yells, "No!"

A swish of air behind me captures my attention, and then pain explodes in my back, sending me to my knees. The magic-charged air surrounding me crackles as both of my wings fall to the ground.

"I stopped her from aging us anymore!" Schafer shouts in triumph and raises his bloody sword.

"You stupid idiot!" Peter snarls as he climbs to his feet. "Now we can't make her keep us young!"

His admission creates a rumble of gasps in the crowd.

Elijah kicks Schafer in the stomach, sailing him into the platform. His sword flies free from his hand and embeds into the side of the stump like some invisible force has taken over.

Elijah kneels by my side. "Lilly?" he asks as he gently pulls me into his grasp.

"The captain must still pay for his crimes on the high seas!" the greasy bald man on the platform yells over the rumbling crowd, trying to continue this bogus execution.

Elijah looks up at him. "And what crimes are those? Searching the world for hidden treasures with my crew?" He points his stub of an arm at Peter. "The crew that that little shit murdered for his twisted enjoyment?"

The little man's brow creases at Peter. "You told me he pillaged and raped and wiped entire cities off the map." His voice cracks.

The crowd murmurs around us. People look at each other with uncertainty and then at the men who were only children just moments ago.

"Peter is a liar," I say from Elijah's arms and look up at the man who could still steal Elijah from me. "He has abused me for years, and he threw me to the crocodiles when I refused to use my magic to kill. Elijah saved me, and it cost him his hand."

Talking takes all my energy, and I slump into the captain's arms.

Captain Hook glances down at me and then back at Peter. "She's the only reason I didn't meet the same demise as my crew. He threw a caged fae into the ocean knowing if the crocodile didn't kill her, the water would."

"Is this true?" the man asks Peter.

Peter shakes his head, but he can't quite bring his eyes up to meet the man's gaze.

"Yes!" a hooded figure in the back calls out and moves slowly through the crowd, limping with a crutch. Wood bumps on the ground. It's the same voice that questioned the captain's crimes. He throws his hood back. A stocky gray-haired man who looks strikingly like the captain stands tall, despite his peg leg and crutch. He glares at the crowd surrounding us and points his crutch at the boys, singling each of them out. "These are the boys who murdered the crew aboard the *Joli Rouge*."

Elijah stares at the man with his mouth hanging open.

"Sorry I didn't get here sooner, Captain." He motions to his leg.

"Who are you?" the little man demands.

"I am Quartermaster Isaiah Hook. The captain's brother." His face reddens as he scans the boys who are now aged men. "I thought I was the lone survivor until I heard rumors that the captain had been sentenced to die today." He wags his pointer finger at Elijah. "This man has not pillaged a village. As a matter of fact, he has revived dying sea towns with the gold and silver we have unearthed."

The little man on the stage sneers at Elijah's brother and crosses his arms. "So, he has never run a sword through a man?"

Isaiah glances at Elijah.

"My sword has made a swift end to rapists and murderers and thieves,"

Elijah says as he stares at Peter. "I do not profess to be an innocent the way she is." He juts his chin at me. "One who they terrorized daily and left near death probably more times than any of us can count." His grip on me tightens. "Look at them. Cutting off her wings stopped their aging process. What you see is a reasonably accurate representation of just how long they've locked up a fae. And those bastards made her keep them young enough to be overlooked by the law."

"She cursed them," the little man on stage says, unwilling to see the truth.

Then it occurs to me that the little man has been bought and paid by the lost boys. He does their bidding, just as I have bent to their will all these years.

"I did not curse them. All I did was take my magic back, and they maimed me because they wanted to be forever young." I wave at the bloody wings on the ground beside me. "They cut off my wings and nullified my magic. This is what they promised—no, threatened me with—daily."

"And you expect this town to believe a fae and two pirates over a group of upstanding citizens of Neverland whom you have turned into old men?" He scoffs at us and turns to the guards. "Grab him."

Before they can even take a step, a clap of thunder rumbles in the clear sky above us. Then a lightning bolt hits the ground in front of Elijah and me, creating a wall of smoke that surrounds us like a protective barrier.

The king of the fae decked out in his armor and adornments rises in all his glory, towering over the square in a form that is larger than life. He points to the small man on the stage, singling him out.

"You have the audacity to question the honesty of a fae?" His voice rumbles like the thunder above. Wind whips around the square with the power of a hurricane making landfall.

The little man's pants darken, and his cheeks turn ruddy with fear. He moves his head back and forth quickly.

"I…I didn't mean to." He puts his hands out to placate the fae king. "I-I'm sorry," he squeals and runs for the safety of the building they dragged Elijah out of.

The entire square cowers as the fae king turns his back on the platform. His gaze moves to Captain Hook and drops to his decapitated limb. He reaches into his pocket and pulls out the captain's severed hand with the watch he's been searching for, still attached just below where it's severed.

"Imagine my surprise when I found *this* inside that hideous beast." He tosses the hand to Captain Hook.

Elijah catches his hand and magic blasts into him from the severed appendage, connecting it back where it belongs. He stares at his regenerated hand as it turns from gray to the color of his flesh, and then he wiggles his fingers, letting out a laugh of disbelief.

My gaze jumps between his healed hand and my father. Fae royalty doesn't just dole out magical favors on a whim. Nor do they look at humans as if they are family, like the way he is looking at Elijah.

The captain's watch shimmers with a fae beacon. Things snap into place, and I meet my father's warm gaze. It soothes my severed soul as much as Elijah's arms do.

My father sent Captain Hook to find his lost treasure.

The king's gaze drops to my severed wings, and the warm moment turns frigid with his fury. The storm gathers around us as he turns to the boys now encased in bodies of old men.

"These are the heathens who imprisoned my daughter?" he asks the captain.

"Yes, my lord," Elijah says and bows his head in respect as if he has been in my father's employment all his life.

My mind drifts to his conversation about being in the fae realm, and again, I wonder what he did.

The king snaps his fingers, bringing Peter's pet crocodile into the square. The crowd gasps, pushing backwards to a safe distance.

Peter points at us as if ordering the beast to attack, but the crocodile smiles in a way that sends a fiery trail of fear up my back. He is no longer Peter's to order around. That much is clear, but it does not seem to register with Peter yet.

I shift and wince at the pain in my back. Elijah's grip on me tightens.

More crocodiles appear, surrounding the boys, herding them into a tight circle. It's only now that Peter realizes he is facing his death and that he no longer has fae magic in his pocket to get him out of it. His eyes widen, knowing that whatever comes next, it will be incredibly painful.

The king looks out at the crowd. "Witness true justice, and understand that crossing a fae comes with swift and often violent ramifications."

Before he can unleash the crocodiles, I blurt out, "Let them live, Father."

He spins toward me with his eyebrows arching. "This is fae justice for stealing you from our sight. For enslaving you and severing your magic." He waves at my bloody wings.

I glance at the pitiful gathering in the square's center. Twelve old men cling to each other with shaking legs and terror in their ancient eyes.

"Death is an end to their punishment."

My words seem to sink in beyond my father's fury, and he tilts his head and nods for me to continue.

"They do not have their youth or my magic to hide behind any longer. Do you not see? Their lives are brief already, and stealing their misery and replacing it with a swift death isn't punishment enough!"

He takes a deep breath and then blows it out through his nose, sending shockwaves through the square, knocking a few of the boys to their knees. My father's gaze narrows, and an evil glint flashes in his eyes.

"Where do they reside?" His voice is filled with malicious intent.

The crocodiles vanish, and I point to the hill above the town square and the only sprawling house gracing the bluff.

The biggest lightning bolt I have ever seen slams into it, turning it to dust.

"You asshole!" Peter cries and turns to the crowd. "You're going to let them get away with this?"

"You are no longer welcome in Neverland!" someone yells back, and the rumblings agree with the lone cry.

Peter's expression darkens, and he turns his angry eyes on me. Pointing, he growls, "This isn't over."

I climb to my feet and stand tall despite the debilitating pain in my back. I stare him down. "It is over, old man. If you ever dare to come within ten feet of me or the captain, I will have you run through like the pig you are." I lift my chin in defiance.

"I should have killed you instead of chopping your wings off," Schafer growls from behind Peter.

It seems the dimwit forgot who is standing by my side.

A lightning bolt turns him to ash.

"I suggest you leave," my father says through teeth that grind with the wrath filling him. "Before I decide that the rest of you deserve the same fate despite my daughter's logical plea."

The boys' heads jerk up from staring at the ash pile where their friend had been standing.

"D-daughter?" Bo asks with a hitch in his voice.

"Yes. You imprisoned the fae king's daughter," Elijah growls at him. "And if I had any say in your sentence, I would strike you down myself."

Peter is the only one that lingers longer than a blink. The rest scurry away as fast as their old legs will take them, which isn't fast at all. Watching the geriatrics leave satisfies my deep-seated anger. Even as Peter storms away, it's in slow motion, and I almost laugh at the irony.

My father turns to us, and his sad eyes take in my mutilated form that I am now locked in, thanks to Schafer's sword. "I cannot bring you home without your magic."

My gaze drops to the ground, and I nod. Without magic, I will not survive the transition to my world. The ley line would identify me as a fallen fae and strike me down for trying to enter the fae realm. It's a protection that was set by the ancients to keep the dark ones from destroying our realm. All fae have a magical signature, or in my case, a magical echo, and without wings, I won't live through the barrier's attack. A human doesn't have any magical signature and will pass through on the will of a fae.

My father tilts my chin up and he gently kisses my cheek. His magic floods through me straight to my injuries, healing what ails me.

"As long as you are with the captain, I will be able to find you." He eyes Elijah. "You are to take care of my daughter as if she is your most prized possession."

Elijah smirks and glances at me. "With pleasure, my lord." He bows.

My father's eyes narrow as he looks between us, and then he decides not to test us further. "Your debt is now paid. You are no longer on my payroll," he adds and then disappears into a cloud of smoke, followed by a clap of thunder that rumbles the ground beneath our feet.

I touch Elijah's hand and the fae watch around his reattached wrist. "So that's why you were adamant about finding that damn crocodile?"

He nods and gives me a half-hearted shrug. "I couldn't notify your father that I found you without it. But it seems something in the crocodile's belly triggered it, anyway."

That thought makes my skin break out in bumps, and I shiver with the chill his words produce. Elijah puts his arm around me and pulls me to his side as he looks around at the people still crowding the edges of the area. He heads to the town docks and his boat that sits waiting for him and his crew.

"You were bound by your debts to find me?" I ask as the crowd parts for us as if we are royalty. I guess in their eyes we are. I smile and nod my thanks for their support as we walk past.

Elijah inhales and nods before glancing at me. "Yes."

"Why?"

"Because I was once young and stupid and attempted to steal the fae king's crown." His cheeks turn crimson as he avoids my gaze.

I blink like I can't believe it, and then my memory rushes back to when I was younger and there was a commotion at the palace. Word came through that a human boy tried to steal my father's crown. My eyes widen at the memory. My father dragged the boy across realms, and I remember clearly the terror in that child's eyes as they met mine.

At that moment, he stole my breath away. The fear in his eyes turned to something else. Something like hope, and he sent me an impish grin that haunted my dreams for decades. It was the only time I saw the human boy.

I stare into Elijah's eyes, the same eyes that left me breathless that first encounter and every encounter thereafter. "That was *you*?"

The tilt of his lips warms me. "I have been searching for you since that day in the fae court."

I ignore his heartwarming words and wave at his form. He should be older than the lost boys at this point.

His brother approaches us slowly, looking more like what I envision Elijah should be like.

Elijah focuses on his brother, stepping away from me to give him a hug. When he pulls away, he turns to me. "Lilly, this is my younger brother, Isaiah."

He bows. "Your grace," he says, keeping his gaze on the ground. He takes off the cloak he wears and offers it to me.

"Thank you." I take the cape and swing it around to wrap around me before looking at Elijah again. "How?" I demand.

I'm not in the mood to be handed over to another trickster.

"I served my sentence in the prisons below the palace and then became your father's gopher. By then, you and your sister had run away, and eventually he started confiding in me." He laughs. "It's the damnedest thing. Your father and I became friends. He trained me in sword fighting and other hand-to-hand combat, and then when I reached the age you see me at now, he made me a deal. He offered me immortality if I would come to this realm and find you." He taps my nose. "*You.* The princess I dreamed of every night since I first saw your beautiful face. It wasn't hard to agree to that deal."

My knees weaken with his words, but he wraps his arm around my waist, keeping me steady, and looks out at the crowd who has not yet dispersed. They seem to enjoy the show.

Elijah clears his throat. "It seems I'm in need of a few crew members. So, anyone who would like to sail with us, come to the dock before sunset." He glances at his brother. "Lead the way, Isaiah."

"Isn't it bad luck to have a woman aboard?" Isaiah asks as he looks between the two of us.

Elijah laughs at his brother. "Not if said lady is my wife."

"You're married?" Isaiah asks with such disbelief that Elijah laughs even harder at his brother.

"Not yet. But we will be before we set sail this evening."

"Oh, you think so?" I say to him as I plant my hands on my hips.

"Yes. And then we can start our own adventure." Elijah pulls me against him and winces. "But that may need to wait until I heal," he adds as he looks down at his bruised chest.

It's my turn to laugh. "I think I'd like to start my adventure right away." I press against him, and he groans in the back of his throat, but he doesn't pull away.

I swipe my lips across his.

Sailing into the sunset every night is going to be an adventure of a lifetime, especially with Captain Elijah Hook at my side.

The End

If you enjoyed A FRACTURED FAIRY TALE: BOOKS 1-10, please consider leaving a review!

Find more books by J.E. Taylor on her website: http://books.jetaylor75.com/

About J.E. Taylor

J.E. Taylor is a USA Today bestselling author, a publisher, an editor, a manuscript formatter, a mother, a wife, a business analyst, and a Supernatural fangirl. Not necessarily in that order. She first sat down to seriously write in February of 2007 after her daughter asked:

"Mom, if you could do anything, what would you do?"

From that moment on, she hasn't looked back.

Besides being co-owner of Novel Concept Publishing, Ms. Taylor also moonlights as a Senior Editor of Allegory, an online venue for Science Fiction, Fantasy and Horror. J.E. Taylor is also one of the co-hosts of the popular podcast <u>Spilling Ink</u>.

She lives in New Hampshire with her husband and two children and during the summer months enjoys her weekends on the shore in southern Maine.

Visit her at https://JETaylor75.com and sign up for her newsletter for early previews of her upcoming books!

If you liked HOOK, you might also like these other fairy tales and magical romance stories from J.E. Taylor's backlist:

A FRACTURED FAIRY TALE

BOOKS 1-10

Little Red Riding Hood, Cinderella, Brave, Rapunzel, Frozen, Snow White, Sleeping Beauty, Aladdin, Beauty and the Beast and Peter Pan – all fairy tales you know and love, but twisted, fractured into something new.

Shifters and magic claw through the pages of these fractured fairy tales, giving you a thrilling take on an old tale.

Will the heroine survive whatever the evil villain has in store? Or will Love conquer all?

Grab your hardcover edition of A Fractured Fairy Tale—books 1-10 and find out!

A Fractured Fairy Tale books 1-10 includes

Red, Cinder, Brave, Tangled, Frozen, Snow, Spindle, Jasmine, Belle, Hook

Find these titles and other fantasy and suspense titles on J.E. Taylor's website!

www.JETaylor75.com